Everything Happens on Mondays

NICOLA DAVIES

First Publication—1995
Second Publication—1998
Third Publication—2003

ISBN I 85902 298 7

This book is published with the support of the Arts Council of Wales.

Printed in Wales at
Gomer Press, Llandysul, Ceredigion

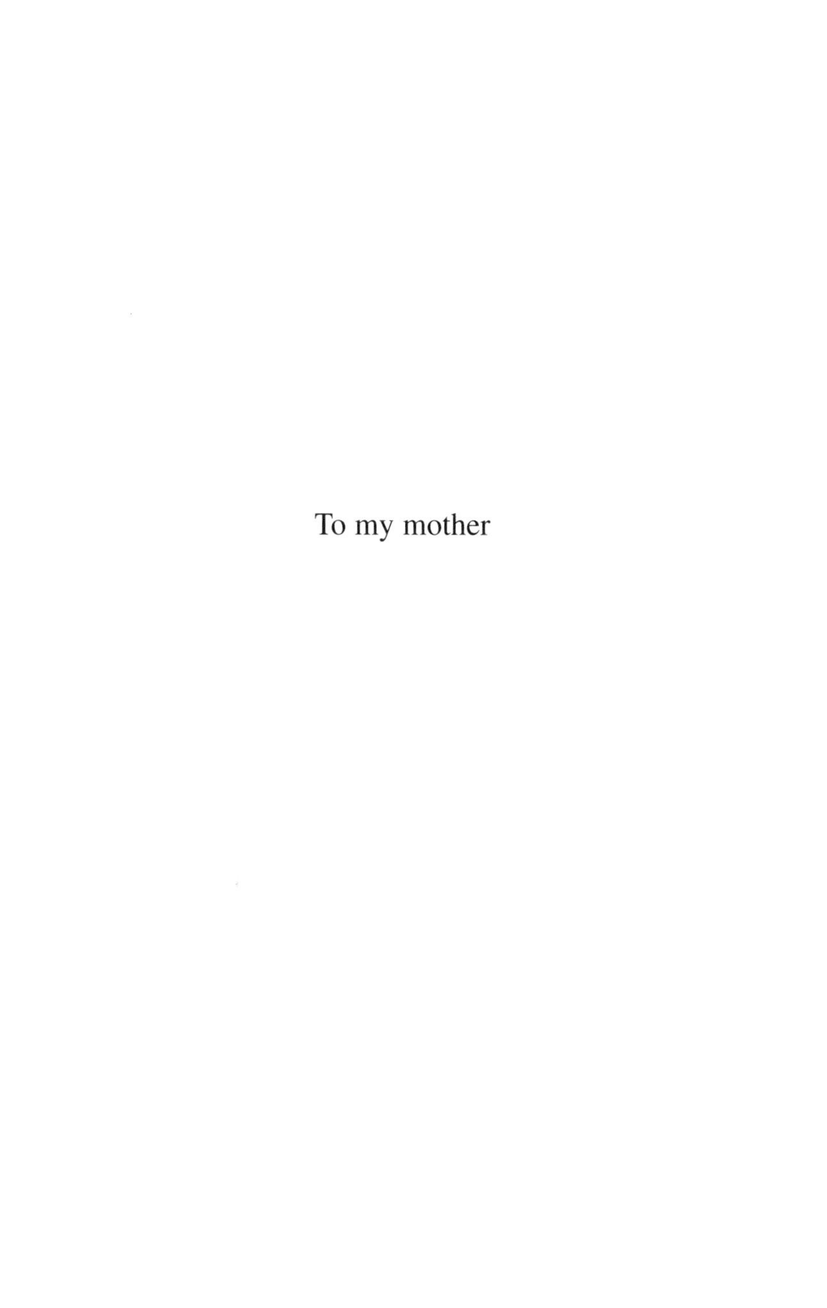

To my mother

CONTENTS

WELCOME TO GLANTWRCH MIDDLE SCHOOL

'Per Glantwrch ad Astra'.

Glantwrch Middle School stands on a hilltop, overlooking the sleepy hamlet of Glantwrch. Surrounded by woodland, the environs of the school provide the ideal setting for young minds and bodies to develop. The children of today are the citizens of tomorrow, says Headmaster Maxwell Beynon. Under his aegis, the school provides training for life, educational and vocational.

Prospective parents requiring appointments with headmaster Maxwell Beynon (Bachelor of Education) please contact the Headmaster's Secretary forthwith.

Top of the Hill

Dai Rix says the school was built on a hill so that children would arrive there out of breath and be fit for nothing but schoolwork. But we hardly notice the steep climb; it's the teachers who start the day breathless.

I call for Andrea Williams on my way to school. If she's still feeding her baby sister, Leah, I take over, for Andrea to take her Mum up a cup of tea. Andrea shouts up, 'Remember to change the baby,' as we leave the house.

Halfway up the hill, Ceri and Columbus join us. Columbus is so pleased to see everyone, his tail's like a demented windscreen wiper. Ceri talks to Columbus like he understands every word. He tells Columbus, 'You behave yourself while I'm in school,' and Columbus barks once for 'Yes'. When we get to the school gates, Ceri says, 'Right, Columbus, I'm going in now. You go straight home.' Columbus barks once, turns and trots off.

Someone in a mauve cardigan races past us. It's Merco Rigger, fresh from his paper round and ready for anything. He races into school to report to Mrs Griffiths, the Head of Year.

We stop before going into the building, and take some deep breaths. It's not that the hill has got to us, more like needing a moment to prepare for what we're about to receive.

'Shall we go in now?' I ask Andrea.

'May as well,' says Andrea, 'no sense waiting any longer.'

She pushes the front doors open and we are swept up into the bloodstream of Glantwrch Middle School.

Mr. Beynon and the Vandal

A large orange leaf presses against the window like a giant hand. I look through its fingers to where empty crisp packets mingle with autumn leaves down in the playground. Beyond the playground is Mr Beynon, the Headmaster; he's watching the teachers' car park through a pair of binoculars.

Inside, we're in English with Mrs Shearer. I'm by the window, watching the Headmaster and listening to the class. We've been reading this book about a nuclear attack and how this family's stuck in the living-room, waiting till it's safe to go out. They discover, too late, that dust has been falling down the chimney and into their drinking-water.

'A little bit of dust never harms nobody,' says Emma Leyshon.

'It's not ordinary dust,' says Ceri Evans, 'it's nucular.'

'Wha?' says Emma.

'New-queue-lar dust,' says Ceri, slowly.

'An' what's that when it's at home?' says Dai Rix.

‘Dust outa the sky,’ says Ceri. Under his school uniform, he’s wearing a purple T-shirt with MUSCLEMAN printed on it in big yellow letters.

‘Ordinary dust just falls down,’ says Emma, like she really knows. She’s swinging her feet back and forth, like she’s a clock.

‘And I suppose new-clear dust falls sideways, does it?’ says Andrea.

Mr Beynon’s binoculars are fixed on the car park. I follow his gaze and see someone hiding among the cars. It’s Rhodri Rhys, huddled inside his duffle coat, watching autumn leaves riding the wind. I’ve been wondering why he wasn’t in the lesson. Now I’m wondering what he’s doing in the car park. As I watch, I see Mr Beynon tiptoeing across the yard, making straight for Rhodri. I try to warn him, but he won’t look up. Suddenly, Mr Beynon appears from behind a car, grabs at Rhodri’s hood and yanks him out of sight.

‘The Headmaster’s got Rhodri!’ I tell Andrea, but she’s not listening. She’s chewing at her bottom lip, deep in her own thoughts. Been acting funny all week, has Andrea, and won’t say why.

‘Right,’ says Mrs Shearer. ‘Let’s get down to work. I want you to design a poster to tell people what to do in the event of a nuclear attack.' She goes on to say we have to write instructions like SEAL ALL DOORS AND WINDOWS and DO NOT PANIC, and draw posters to illustrate them.

'Find a partner,' she says, 'and plan the poster between you.'

'My partner's not here,' says Dai. 'Where's Rhodri Rhys?'

'He was feeling sick,' says Mrs Shearer. 'I said he could go out for some fresh air. He should be back any minute.'

'The Headmaster's got him,' I say, but no-one's listening; they're too busy finding partners and paper and tables to work on.

Andrea pairs up with Pietro, because he's the only one who can draw. Emma Leyshon picks me to share her 24 coloured pencils: six each of yellow, red, blue and green. While Dai's waiting for Rhodri, he wanders from desk to desk, nicking things.

'What's that you've drawn?' he says, poking his fingers at our poster.

'What d'you think it is, Dai?' says Emma, proudly.

'Looks like a tree,' he says, putting a blue in his pocket.

'It's a mushroom cloud,' says Emma.

'More like an oak tree,' says Dai, picking up a red to go with the blue.

'Why don't you start on your poster?' says Emma. 'Rhodri'll be along any minute,' and she holds her hand out for the coloured pencils.

'No, he won't,' I say at last. 'The Headmaster's got him.' I've been waiting so long, the words come out in a rush.

'Got Rhodri? Where? Why didn't you say before?' says Dai. He reaches in his pocket and gives Emma back the coloured pencils.

I don't get a chance to answer, because the door opens. The Headmaster comes in, steering Rhodri by the shoulder. Rhodri's feet are pumping the floor and his cheeks are pale.

'You were right,' says Emma. 'It is the 'Edmasta with Rhodri.'

'Good afternoon, class,' he booms at us.

We put our colouring down and chant 'Good Afternoon, Mr Beynon' in the sing-song fashion teachers like. Even Rhodri joins in.

Mr. Beynon squeezes Rhodri's shoulder till he squeaks. Rhodri's face is white now, and he's trying not to cry.

'I found this scallywag in the teachers' car park, Mrs Shearer,' says Mr Beynon. 'He even informed me that you had given him permission to be there. To take deep breaths, he said. BREATHING! Scratching, more like.'

'Scratching, Mr Beynon?' says Mrs Shearer.

Mr Beynon scans the room to ensure we're getting on with our work. We all start colouring like mad. Blue mushrooms, green people.

'Scratching cars, Mrs Shearer,' says the Headmaster, raising his voice and aiming it at the class. 'I discovered a scratch on the school minibus last week. Since when, I have been surveying the teachers' car park. Today, my patience has been rewarded. My surveillance has reaped fruit in the shape of Rhodri Rhys He thought he was safe, that no-one could see him. Little did he reckon with my binoculars. Vandals, beware.' He shakes Rhodri by the hood several times.

'Rhodri's not a vandal,' says Mrs Shearer. 'I can't believe he's been scratching cars,' she says. 'He wouldn't do a thing like that.'

'I asked him what he was doing there and all he would say was thinking,' says Mr Beynon.

'Rhodri, tell Mr Beynon what you were doing in the car park.' Mrs Shearer smiles at Rhodri. He takes a deep breath, opens his mouth, looks at the Headmaster's stern expression and says nothing. Mr Beynon glares at us to get on with our work.

We colour away. The nuclear posters are beginning to look like firework night.

'Rhodri had not yet begun to perpetrate this mindless act of vandalism,' says the Headmaster. 'I nipped his intention in the bud, Mrs Shearer.' He squeezes Rhodri's shoulder again and Rhodri obliges him with a squeak. 'That is to say,' says Mr Beynon, 'I caught him before he had the chance to do anything.'

'He wasn't intending to do anything to the cars, I'm sure of it,' says Mrs Shearer. 'Tell the Headmaster, Rhodri.'

Rhodri does his drowning fish impression again.

'This time there will be no reprisals.' Mr Beynon stops and grimaces at the class before proceeding. 'Should I find Rhodri or any other pupil in the teachers' car park, near MY CAR, there will be trouble. In future, vandals like Rhodri will receive a year's continuous detention.' He looks round at our shocked expressions and adds, 'Twelve entire months. The culprit will not leave the school premises for a whole year.' He glares at us, gives Rhodri a last squeeze, and goes out.

'He can't keep us in school for a year, can he?' says Ceri Evans.

‘Where would we sleep?’ says Emma.

‘Who would feed all my animals?’ says Ceri, with just a fleck of panic in his voice.

‘They have to give you warning,’ says Dai. ‘My Nan says.’

‘Mr Beynon didn’t mean it,’ says Andrea. ‘He’d have to live in the school for an entire year, wouldn’t he? No-one’s going to stay in a school a whole year.’

‘Of course they’re not,’ says Mrs Shearer. She looks hard at Rhodri. ‘I don’t understand why you didn’t answer the Headmaster, Rhodri. You didn’t scratch any cars, did you?’

‘Course not,’ says Rhodri. ‘I’m not a vandal.’

‘Then why didn’t you explain that to the Headmaster, Rhodri,’ asks Mrs Shearer, gently. ‘Why didn’t you tell him ?’

We all wait on Rhodri’s answer. We’re all wondering why he hasn’t protested his innocence.

‘I didn’t dare tell him,’ says Rhodri, ‘in case he put me in detention. You see, Miss, I’ve just been sick all over the boot of his car.’

Merco the Messenger

Merco Rigger. The only boy in Middle School to wear a mauve cardigan and socks three sizes too big. Merco the messenger. Turn a corner and there he is, knocking at the Head's door to deliver a sealed envelope, or winging his way across the playing field that links us with the High School. I suppose he must go to lessons occasionally, but the only time I ever see him is on his rounds, socks flapping at his ankles. Always cheerful is Merco; always alone.

We're coming out of Maths one day, when he yells after us down the corridor, 'Andrea Williams and Nia Markham, Mrs Eleri Griffiths wants to see you in her room at break.' He's short, even for Year Seven, is Merco, with freckles like ink-blots. We wait for him to catch us up.

'What's she want?' says Andrea.

'I'm just the messenger,' says Merco, racing off to deliver the next one.

So there we are, knocking on Mrs G's door, ready with a bunch of all-occasion excuses.

'Come in,' she says, indicating two chairs. She's smiling at us, so I relax, but I see Andrea's still not too happy. 'Well, girls, how's school these days?'

'All right, Miss,' says Andrea, warily.

I just nod. She doesn't want to hear about the state of the girls' toilets or how Samantha Thomas won't be friends with me any more.

'Now girls,' she says when we're all sitting down, 'I won't keep you long. I want you to do me a favour.'

You should see the look on Andrea's face.

'A new girl is joining us next week. From Bristol. It's not very pleasant joining a class in mid-term. I'd like you two to look after her for me. Just until she settles in.'

I'm about to ask what this new girl's name is, when Andrea butts in. 'Why us?' she asks. 'Her parents are divorced, aren't they?' And she looks Mrs Griffiths straight in the eyes.

'Well, yes, they are,' says Mrs Griffiths. 'Her mother's moving down here from Bristol with Julie-Ann. How very astute of you, Andrea.'

'Not 'stewt at all,' says Andrea. 'It's not right, Miss. Why do you always ask for us two when it's divorce?'

Mrs Eleri Griffiths's smile's a little lop-sided now.

'Well it's not fair to class us all together,' says

Andrea. 'Nia and me's not friends just because our parents split up.' Then she stops, as if she was suddenly wondering why exactly we are friends.

I'm expecting Mrs Griffiths to give Andrea a row, but she thinks for a minute, then gives Andrea a proper smile, like she's a real person. 'You're right, of course, Andrea,' she says. 'I won't do it again.'

'Why don't you ask Merc?' says Andrea. 'His Dad don't live at home, do he? Let Merco Rigger look after the new girl.' She grins at the thought. 'He can take her on a tour of the school, Miss, when he does his messages.'

Just then, there's a knock at the door, and who should come in but Merco Rigger. We all burst out laughing. Merc looks at us, then joins in the laughter. He's alright, Merc is. Good-natured. He's wearing that mauve cardigan of his sister's again. There's a button missing.

'Done 'em all,' he says to Mrs Griffiths. 'What now?'

'Mrs Griffiths wants you to look after a new girl for her,' says Andrea, casually. 'Wants you to help her settle in. Take her out to the chippie.'

'Joker,' says Merc, raising his ginger eyebrows, and shoots out of the room so fast that his socks flap double-time.

'You've embarrassed him, Andrea', says Mrs Griffiths. Poor little Mercury.'

Dylan's his real name, Dylan Rigger. She calls him Mercury because 'Mercury is the messenger of the Gods'. When she told us, Andrea whispered, 'Flatters herself, don't she?'

Monday morning comes and Mrs Griffiths brings Julie-Ann to registration, to introduce her to the class. She's short, blonde and blue-eyed with a watery smile. Merc's jaw drops when he sees her.

'Look at Merc. Can't take his eyes off her,' Andrea whispers, adding, 'first time he's ever seen anyone shorter than him.'

We're all surprised when Merco troops in to first lesson with us. Maths teacher can't get over it. 'And who is this little stranger we have among us?' asks Mrs Flynn.

'Julie-Ann Bassett,' says Andrea. 'She's from Bristol.'

'Not Julie-Ann,' says Mrs Flynn. 'I mean the little stranger sitting at the back of the room.'

We all turn round to gawp, but it's only Merc. He grins and asks her for some paper and a pencil.

After break, he's got some messages to do, but

you can tell his heart's not in it, the way he's walking instead of speeding along. He tries to join us for French, but Dai Llewellyn's not having it. 'Wait out there, boy, until I'm ready for you,' he booms. He makes Merco wait outside the room all lesson. Funny thing, Merco doesn't try anything on; he just waits outside till the bell goes.

When we come out from French, he follows us down the corridor.

'Trying to get yourself an education at last, boy?' says Andrea, gruffly, taking off the Headmaster, even to the way he twitches his nose. Merc doesn't answer her; he's only got eyes for Julie-Ann.

'I think he fancies you,' says Andrea to Julie-Ann.

'Who?' says Julie-Ann, all innocence.

'Him,' says Andrea, 'little Merc there.'

Julie-Ann turns to look at Merco. He gives her a big friendly grin. Julie-Ann looks him up and down, then fixes her gaze on his feet. She turns to Andrea. 'Look at his socks,' she says, as if there's an exam in SOCKS and Merco's just failed it.

There's a long silence.

'What did you say?' says Andrea, fierce-like.

Julie-Ann backs off. 'Nothing,' she mumbles.

'Don't lie,' says Andrea.' I heard you.'

'I didn't say anything, did I?' says Julie-Ann, turning to me; I turn away.

All this time, Merc's just standing there. 'It's all right,' he says at last. He looks at Julie-Ann and grins. 'I've got two other pairs like this at home,' he says. Julie-Ann does not return his smile.

Andrea puts an arm round Merc. 'Merco,' she says, 'she's not for you. Put your tongue back in your head, mun.'

But Merc looks at Julie-Ann. 'What if I wear a proper pair of socks?'

She looks at him. 'You never know,' she says.

"What else would you like me to do?' says Merc.

'No cardigans, neither,' says Julie-Ann.

'And then you'll go out with me?'

'I might,' she says.

I can see that Andrea's getting ready to thump her, but there's no need.

Merc looks at Julie-Ann and raises his eyebrows. 'Can't change the socks,' he says, 'they're me father's. End of message.' He turns and races off down the corridor, his socks flapping top-speed.

'Good for you, Merc,' says Andrea, quietly. We watch till he's out of sight. 'C'mon,' she says, taking my arm. We leave Julie-Ann standing there on her own in the corridor.

Merco Rigger. Always cheerful. Always alone.

Emma's Future

Emma Leyshon wasn't bothered about her future until she found a lost puppy in her Gran's coalshed and the local paper wrote about her discovery. She was a changed person. One day she was playing football with us in the park and getting splattered with mud; the next, she had her hair permed and covered her fingernails in pink polish. Suddenly, she couldn't pass a mirror without smiling in it.

'Been in a fight?' Andrea asks her one morning. 'Got a black eye?'

'It's my eyeshadow,' says Emma. 'It's called Jetty.'

'Been eating blackberries?' says Andrea.

'Don't be silly,' says Emma. 'You know it's lipstick.'

'Why all the clownpaint?' says Andrea.

'In case there's a photographer about,' Emma explains.

'In the playground?' says Andrea.

'You never know,' says Emma.

'You coming to play football with us after school?' says Andrea

'No thanks. It might bruise my legs,' says Emma. 'My mum says my legs are one of my best features.'

Police Constable Parry's coming to talk to us in Social Studies, and Emma and I are to meet him. We're walking along the corridor to the car park, and she's practising her welcome speech. 'Good morning, Police Constable Parry. Welcome to Glantwrch Middle School. I'm Emma Leyshon and this is Nia. Please come with us.' She says it over and over again.

Mr Beynon, the Headmaster, is outside his room, cleaning a message off the wall. He waves us down with his cleaning rag. 'An opportune moment,' he booms at us. 'Just the job for two energetic young ladies.'

'We can't stop,' says Emma, stopping. 'We're meeting a visitor, me and Nia. Mrs Griffiths is going to take photographs for the school magazine.' She flashes him a half-smile; no sense wasting a full one.

'Visitor?' he says, staring at the half-erased message, ** OFF, BEYNON. He squirts paint remover at the wall, and works away at it furiously with the cleaning rag.

We wait for Police Constable Parry in the foyer, opposite the car park.

Emma's still practising her welcome speech: 'Good morning, Police Constable Parry. Welcome to Glantwrch Middle School.' She turns to me. 'You can say the bit about Welcome to Glantwrch Middle School, if you like. Then I'll say my name, then you say yours, then I'll say the rest.'

'You can say it all, if you like,' I say.

She takes out her eye make-up and does her eyes. 'What do you think?' she says. 'Think they'll look good in the photograph? It's for my portfolio.'

'Your what?'

'My portfolio. For when I'm a model. My mum's keeping a scrapbook of my news cuttings.'

'But you've only got one news cutting,' I say. 'And that's got MISSING PUPPY FOUND AT LAST above it.'

'My Mum says my face will be on all the magazine covers one day,' says Emma. 'There you'll be serving in Spar and when people buy a magazine, you'll say, "That's Emma Leyshon. I went to school with her."'

Mr Beynon's coming towards us with a cloth in one hand and Dai Rix's ear in the other. He tells Dai to polish the glass doors, then the handles. 'Visitor,' he mutters as he walks off.

'What's he on about?' says Dai.

'Social Studies,' says Emma. 'Police Constable Parry's coming to talk to us. We're meeting him, me and Nia. Then I'm having my photograph taken with him for the school magazine. Full-length. I've got the legs for it.'

'Same legs you had when you was a sheep in the Infants' Nativity Play?' says Dai. 'Or was it a giraffe?'

When Police Constable Parry arrives, Emma runs out and introduces herself.

'Good Morning, Police Constable Parry. I'm Emma Leyshon. I'm to take you to the classroom. We're all looking forward to having our photos taken with you.' And she marches him past me down the corridor.

'They've gone without you,' says Dai.

'Obviously,' I say, waiting for her to look back. She doesn't.

When Dai and I arrive at class, PC Parry's talking about his schooldays. He says he wasn't an angel by any means and all he'd cared about was sport. He'd even had a trial for Swansea City. 'I just wasn't good enough to be a professional footballer,' he said.

'Were you gutted?' asked Dai.

'Thought it was the end of the world at the time,' says PC Parry, 'but I play soccer for the

Police Federation now. Everything's worked out fine.'

Andrea asks about opportunities for women in the police force.

'Every opportunity,' says PC Parry. 'There's nothing women can't achieve in the force. Thinking of joining us when you're old enough?'

'I might,' says Andrea.

'I'm going to be a fashion model when I leave school,' says Emma.

'Good for you,' says PC Parry. 'My girlfriend's a model. Very independent lady. Does all her own film processing. And her tax returns.'

'Does she?' says Emma, surprised.

'She's got a science degree', says PC Parry. 'You can't be a successful model without qualifications these days.'

'Can't you?' says Emma, taken aback. 'Do models have to pass exams?' She sounds near to tears. For the rest of the lesson, she just sits there, thinking. She doesn't join us for the photograph.

Afterwards, Emma comes over. 'Are we still friends, Nia and Andrea?'

'Course we are.'

'That was good, wasn't it?' says Andrea. 'I'm going to join the police when I leave school. Are you still going to be a model, Emma?'

'No,' says Emma. 'I didn't know about having to pass exams.' She makes a face at us. Then she smiles. 'Dai's right about me. I do look like a giraffe. Are you playing football after school today? I've missed it.'

When she turns up for football after school, it's the old Emma. No make-up. no fixed smiles. We're so pleased to see her, we forget she's hopeless and say she can choose her position.

'Put me in goal,' says Emma, 'I want to be in goal.'

'Good choice that,' mutters Dai. 'She'll do least harm there.' But this time, when he kicks the ball, Emma saves it. As she does so, there's this flash. Someone's taking photographs.

'It's him,' says Emma. 'The man from the newspaper. MISSING PUPPY.'

'Always on the look-out for a story,' he says, calling us over.

Next day, Emma's photo's in the newspaper. She's sitting on our shoulders, holding the ball and we're all looking up at her, like the photographer told us to. Under the photograph is written

GIRL IN GOAL

by our own correspondent

When it comes to keeping goal, Emma Leyshon is the one to watch. The envy of all the boys in her year, she's a better goalkeeper than any of them. Emma's not only just got her eye on the ball, she's got her eye on a footballing future.

When Emma tells everyone she's going to be a professional footballer, no-one's got the heart to tell her she'll never make it. It's not that she's a girl; it's because she's absolutely hopeless at football.

Columbus to the Rescue

'Smashin' dog, that Columbus,' says Dai. 'Where'd you get him?'

'Found him in the woods, in a carrier bag,' says Ceri, 'with two tins of dogfood.'

'Why is he called Columbus?' asks Emma, tickling Columbus's ears.

'Cause I discovered him.'

'That's the wrong way round,' she says, 'Columbus wasn't discovered.'

'Yes he was,' says Ceri. 'He says he'll never forget it.'

Dai and I exchange smiles, but we don't say anything. We know how Ceri feels about his animals. He thinks they talk to him.

He's got two cats, both marmalade, three hamsters, a grass-snake called Zebedee, and his dappled dog, Columbus. Ceri's Mum likes the cats and the hamsters and she says Zebedee's no trouble, but she's not too keen on Columbus. He's always taking her things and burying them in the garden. If she can't find her purse or her lipstick, she knows to look for them in the garden, among the rosebushes.

One afternoon when we come out of school, Columbus comes to meet us with something in his mouth. He drops it at Ceri's feet.

'Thinks he's a magpie,' says Ceri. 'Always going for shiny things.' He speaks to Columbus, 'What's that you've brought me?'

'Looks like a cigarette lighter,' says Dai.

Ceri bends down and picks it up. 'It is a lighter,' he says. 'Gold.'

'We could sell that to one of the teachers,' says Dai.

'No, we couldn't,' says Ceri, turning it over. 'This is my Dad's birthday present. Got his initials on it. Mam had it done special. We hid it in my wardrobe, so he wouldn't find it.'

'Looks like your dog found it instead,' says Andrea.

Ceri pats Columbus on the head and says, 'Lucky you brought it to me instead of burying it.' Columbus barks a snatch of Morse Code.

'What did he say?' asks Emma. She's the only one of us who thinks Ceri and Columbus really talk to each other.

'He says he found this in a dark hole,' says Ceri.

'Amazing,' says Dai, chewing at a smile, 'it's

amazing the way you understands him. Can he do fractions?'

Ceri puts the lighter in his pocket, after checking there's no holes.

'That's some lighter,' says Dai. 'Gold, eh? Let's have a look at it.' He holds his hand up in the air, for Ceri to throw it.

'Better not,' says Ceri

'I only wants a look,' says Dai. He clicks his fingers to Columbus and Columbus barks at him. 'See,' says Dai, winking at us, 'Columbus said I could look at it. I'll give it straight back.'

'Alright,' says Ceri, 'straight back, mind.' And he throws the lighter for Dai to catch.

One minute, the lighter's in Ceri's hand, the next it's shot past Dai and into the playing field.

'I wasn't ready,' says Dai, automatically.

'Are you ever?' says Andrea.

'Where's it gone?' says Ceri. 'My Mum will bonsai Columbus if we don't find that lighter.'

We search the playing fields on our hands and knees, trying to find the lighter. There's no sign of it.

'I hafta go soon,' says Emma. 'I'll be late for my fitness class. Anyway, we'll never find that lighter. Never.'

'Don't be so daft,' says Andrea. 'Of course we'll find it.'

'Columbus has found something,' says Ceri, as Columbus bounds towards us; he drops a half-eaten cheese sandwich at our feet, then bounds off to find more treasure.

'It's getting dark,' says Dai. 'We'll have to search tomorrow. Don't worry, Ceri; we'll find it. When's your Da's birthday ?'

'Sunday,' says Ceri, looking worried.

'You see,' says Dai, 'plenty of time. We'll find that lighter tomorrow. It can't have gone far.'

Next morning, in the hall, Mrs Cadwalladr's at the piano, waiting for Mr Beynon to start assembly. While she's waiting, she practises hymns silently, fingers hovering above the keys. Mr Beynon comes in and mounts the stage, then shuts his hymn book with a loud clap, to catch our attention. Mrs Cadwalladr plays a chord, footing away at the pedals like she's riding a bike uphill.

Mr Beynon steps forward. 'Before singing our opening hymn,' he says, 'I have an announcement to make. Today is Lost Property Day. Consequently, there will be an extended lunch-hour for those wishing to retrieve lost or mislaid items.' He makes a clicking sound to show his disapproval. 'The properties which careless individuals have strewn about the school are sweaters, socks, hairbands, purses, combs, gloves, spectacles, computer games, lipsticks, mascara, playing cards, and a gold cigarette lighter.'

'That's your lighter,' Dai tells Ceri. 'Told you it would turn up, didn't I?'

Mr Beynon frowns at Dai, then carries on. 'Hands up those of you who have lost any or all of such glittering prizes.' Every hand in the room shoots up. He frowns again. 'Think before claiming,' he says. 'Think long and hard. In particular, think about claiming lipsticks, playing cards and cigarette lighters Because if you do claim these items, you will have myself and Mrs Cynthia Cadwalladr to contend with. The owners of this forbidden fruit will receive detentions, one detention per item claimed.' He pauses for effect, then carries on. 'In other words, claim at your peril!' He glowers at us all, then nods at Mrs Cadwalladr.

'Now for our hymn,' he announces. 'We shall sing "All things Bright and Beautiful". Turn to page three of your hymn sheets.'

When the bell goes for lunch, we discuss what to do about the lighter.

'Just tell them the truth,' says Pietro.

'The truth?' says Ceri. 'Do you think they'll

believe my dog brought my Dad's cigarette lighter to school?'

At lunch-time, we watch people go into the Lost Property room and come out with found property. Byron claims two combs, Merc comes out with a pair of pink socks and Andrea's reunited with her school sweater.

'What's it like in there?' Dai asks her.

'Beynon's been watching too much T.V,' she says. 'He thinks he's in *The Bill*. First you have to empty your pockets for him to write everything down. Then he makes you describe what you've lost and he writes that down too. Then he lets you look at the Lost Property. If you manage to prove it's yours, he writes down the details in another book. Then you have to sign your name that you've received it.' She looks at Ceri and shakes her head. 'There's no way you'll get that lighter.'

'Yes, there is,' says Ceri, pointing to the playground.

Dai looks out of the window. 'I can't see anything.'

'It's Columbus,' says Ceri. 'He's come to help us.' He opens the window, leans out and whistles. Columbus crosses the playground and jumps in to join us.

'We're in trouble, boy,' says Ceri. 'The lighter's

in there, in the Head's room. You'll have to get it. Andrea will tell you where it is.'

'No, she won't,' says Andrea. 'I'm not giving directions to a dog.'

'Please,' says Ceri.

So she kneels down and talks to Columbus like he's one of us. 'It's at the back of the room on a table,' she says, trying not to laugh. Columbus barks at her, tail wagging away like it's on time and a half.

'Has he got all that?' asks Andrea, 'or is there anything else he needs me to explain? Like percentages?'

'Don't make fun of him, he doesn't like it,' says Ceri. He tells Columbus, 'Now, boy, all you need to do is create a disturbance. Then Emma will dash in and get that lighter.'

'Will I?' says Emma.

'You haven't been in yet,' says Ceri. 'When you do, Columbus will race in after you and distract the Head.'

As soon as Emma goes in to claim some lost property, Ceri pushes Columbus through the door after her with 'Off you go, Columbus'. There's a sudden silence, followed by uproar. Then Mr Beynon runs down the corridor shouting, 'Stop that dog. Stop that dog.'

Suddenly, Columbus races back down the corridor and dives under Mr Beynon's legs. Mr Beynon turns round, and Columbus dashes back under his legs again, then races off towards the main doors. After a minute, Mr Beynon puffs his way towards us, shouting, 'Stop that dog!'

No-one moves.

At hometime, we meet up at the playing-fields.

'Where's Columbus?' askes Andrea.

'I told him to go home,' says Ceri. 'He's not safe round here. And anyway, he's tired out after helping me get the lighter. I'd never have done it without him.'

'What about me?' wails Emma. 'I got the lighter, didn't I?'

'Columbus created the disturbance,' says Ceri, 'didn't he?'

'Columbus did well,' says Andrea, winking at Emma.

'He did get a little carried away, though,' says Ceri. 'He let Emma get the lighter, but he got some treasure for himself, too.'

'What d'you mean?' asks Andrea.

Ceri points to the car park. Mr Beynon's standing by his car, searching his coat pockets.

'I think these are his,' says Ceri, showing us a bunch of keys.

We watch Mr Beynon for a while as he searches under the car; he walks around it, then stands there, looking baffled.

'Let's go home,' says Andrea. 'We'll give him his keys back tomorrow.'

Pietro and Mr Busby

'Where's Flynn off to now?' says Andrea, at the window.

I look down and see our maths teacher, Mrs Shirley Flynn, crossing the playground, her black boots flicking past each other.

Emma joins us and thumps on the rusty window, but Mrs Flynn can't hear her. 'Oy,' shouts Emma. 'We're up here.'

'She must have forgotten,' says Andrea.

'Perhaps she's left the iron on,' says Emma. 'She's gotta race home to turn it off before her house burns down.'

As we watch from the top corridor, she gets into her car and drives away.

'Free lesson,' says Dai Rix, trying to look disappointed and failing.

Byron Huw Tapper can't handle change. He goes over to Pietro. 'Mrs Flynn's gone,' he says. 'We haven't got a teacher.'

'Let's go to class, Byron,' says Pietro. 'I'll give you some work to do.' Pietro's the eldest of five, so he's used to looking after people.

When we get to the classroom, there's a strange

man waiting for us. He's tall and bony and looks like a stick-insect.

'Mrs Flynn's class?' he asks brusquely.

'Thassright,' says Andrea.

'We just seen her in her car,' says Emma.

'Saw her, not seen her,' corrects the man.

'She's left her iron on,' says Emma, 'and the house is on fire.'

'She's gone on a course,' says the man.

'No, she's not,' says Byron Huw Tapper. 'We just seen her.'

'She came for her books,' says the man. 'I'm in charge. March in.'

So we all troop in. The new teacher tells us his name's Dennis Busby. He makes us all chant 'Good Morning, Mr Busby.' We've got a problem about what to call him, because his feet are so big: we're not sure whether to call him Bigfoot or Stick. Andrea looks at me and then at his feet, but I shake my head: I prefer to call him Stick.

'Are you just here for the day, Sir?' asks Emma Leyshon, trying out her two-second grin.

'I'm here for the week,' he says.

'You a student?' says Andrea, innocent-like.

'We 'ad a student in Juniors,' says Emma Leyshon, 'for fractions.'

'I'm not a student,' says Stick, going red.

'You a real teacher?' asks Dai

'I have a first-class degree in Mathematics,' says Stick.

'Good for you, mun,' says Andrea.

He can't stop us talking now.

'Work 'ard, did you, Sir?' says Emma. 'Pass all your GCSEs?'

'Pass your driving test, Sir?' asks Ceri Evans.

We all join in, even me. The Stick tries to answer us all at first, but then he gets nervous-like and starts to wave us back to our seats. When that doesn't work, he yells SIT DOWN. It's a good noise, bit squeaky, but he's got a lot of power for a stick. We sit down, but we don't stop talking.

'Give us a test, Sir,' says Pietro, taking pity. 'That'll keep us quiet.'

'A test,' says Stick, 'yes, we'll have a test.' He gives us all paper and tells us all to write the date, our names and the word TEST.

'Please Sir, do we hafta do the test?' Byron Huw Tapper calls out.

'Of course you do,' says Stick, booming and squeaking together.

Now all the class is worried, Pietro most of all. He'd forgotten about Byron. Byron can't do Maths. He can't do anything. On Tuesdays and Thursdays, Byron's support teacher sits at the back of the class with him, sorting out coloured counters. But this is Monday; on Mondays, Byron copies from Pietro.

'But Sir,' says Byron.

'What's the matter ?' says Stick.

'Nothing,' says Pietro, silencing Byron with a nod. He's not going to tell a stranger that Byron can't read or do sums. 'He's top of the class, Sir,' says Pietro. 'Byron can do everything. Tests are boring for him, Sir.'

'Top of the class,' says Emma, nodding away.

'Top of the class,' echoes Byron, liking the sound of it.

'I don't care if you're top of the school,' says Stick, 'you must do the test with everyone else.' Then he fishes a pair of plastic gloves from his pocket and rolls them carefully over his fingers.

'What are you wearing those for, Sir?' asks Julie-Ann.

'I've an Allergy,' snaps Stick. 'I'm allergic to chalk.'

'My Dad's allergic to bee-stings,' says Ceri Evans.

'My Uncle Griff's allergic to work,' guffaws Dai Rix.

Then Stick blows his top and begins a dance of

despair. He stamps his feet on the floor and waves his hands at us.

'You doing a war-dance, Sir?' says Emma.

'Rain-dance, more like,' says Dai. 'Better stop, Sir, or there'll be showers in here.'

'Better give us that test, Sir,' says Pietro quietly. He smiles at Mr Busby, like he's sorry for all the trouble we're giving him.

Mr Busby writes TEST on the blackboard and underneath it he writes twenty questions for us to answer. We look at the questions. Long multiplication, addings-up. and percentage. We don't know whether to be glad because the test's so easy, or insulted because we can all do it. All but Byron, that is.

Byron whispers something to Pietro.

'Don't worry,' Pietro whispers back.

'No talking,' bawls Mr Busby. 'Get on with your tests.'

Pietro passes his paper to Byron, for Byron to copy the answers and hand it back to Pietro. We try to keep Mr Dennis Busby occupied so he doesn't notice what's happening. We don't want Byron simpled by this first-class Stick.

'When's Mrs Flynn coming back, then?' asks Ceri Evans, adding 'Sir.'

‘Get on with your test,’ says Stick, removing his gloves and sitting in the teacher’s chair.

‘What’ll happen to you when Mrs Flynn comes back?’ asks Emma

‘He’ll be down the dole wone he?’ says Dai, ‘like me Uncle Griff.’

They know how to work him, this lot. He gets quite red in the face and tells them he’s got a job waiting for him in September, at Mumbles Comprehensive.

‘You’ll be with the *crachach* there, mun,’ says Andrea.

But Stick’s not listening. He’s staring at the back of the room, eyes wide, mouth like a haddock’s.

‘You two boys,’ he calls, poking a finger in the air. ‘Yes, you two at the back. Come here, and bring your test papers with you.”

Pietro leads the way He puts his test paper on Mr Busby’s desk, then motions Byron Huw Tapper to follow suit.

Mr Busby takes a paper in each hand and looks from one to the other, comparing. ‘Same right answers,’ he says, ‘and same wrong answers. Identical. You two have been cheating, haven’t you?’

‘Wuzzn’t me,’ says Byron, shaking his head hard.

‘I don’t know what your Mrs Flynn allows,’ says Stick, ‘but I don’t allow cheating. Who’s your Head of Year?’

Now Byron’s really worried: he can’t remember her name.

‘Mrs Eleri Griffiths is our Head of Year,’ says Pietro.

‘Yes,’ says Byron, ‘she is.’

Stick gets a blank piece of paper and writes ‘Mrs Griffiths’. He looks at the two boys. ‘Now I need to know your names.’

Pietro looks at Byron.

‘Sir,’ he says, ‘this is nothing to do with Byron. It’s not Byron’s fault. It’s mine. I made him show me the answers.’

‘Yes,’ says Byron. ‘He made me.’

Stick looks at Byron, then at Pietro and comes to the wrong conclusions. ‘You,’ he says to Byron, ‘sit down. In future, if you know the answers, don’t convey them to other pupils.’

‘No,’ says Byron, ‘I won’t.’ He sits down.

‘The worst sorts of people are those who cheat and lie,’ says Sir.

‘Yessir,’ says Pietro.

‘I mean to inform your parents about this cheating,’ says Stick.

‘No,’ says Emma Leyshon. ‘Not his parents. His Dad’ll belt him.’

‘All the more reason for me to write to him,’ says Sir. He sends Dai Rix for the register so he can copy down Pietro’s address

He must have sent that letter, because Pietro’s Da gave him a right belting for copying from Byron.

Everything Happens on Mondays

'When you puffs your cheeks out,' Dai tells Emma, 'you looks like a chipmunk.'

Emma purses her lips to let the air out. 'Look who's talking,' she says. 'At least it's only when I blows. You always looks like a bullfrog.'

When they asked for volunteers to learn a wind instrument, Andrea grabbed Emma's hand and held it up in the air. Then she did the same with mine.

'What are you doing, Andrea?' says Emma. 'I don't want to play an instrument.'

'Yes, you do,' says Andrea. 'It's a pain getting used to school after the weekend. This'll put some butter on Mondays.'

We knew what she meant: you spend your weekend learning to live without bells and then suddenly they're ringing in your ears every forty-five minutes. That's why everything seems to happen on a Monday: you're just not used to being back at school and you're still expecting everything to make sense.

'Ask to play clarinet,' says Andrea. 'It's the

easiest to play. And lessons are first thing Monday mornings.'

So here we are, three weeks later, still blowing and puffing at the clarinet, and not a sound between us.

'Perhaps she's given us all duff instruments,' said Andrea.

'There's nothing wrong with the clarinets,' says Dai Rix. 'My Gran can play MEN OF MORGANNWG on mine,' he adds mournfully. Dai joined the clarinet group last Monday. His Gran's been on at him to play an instrument for weeks, so she can accompany him on the piano. She says it will do him good not to watch the box all evening.

'I still don't understand what made you join us,' says Emma. 'You even sings like a frog.'

'He fancies Miss Peri,' says Andrea.

'Does he?' says Emma. 'But she's got a moustache.'

'She's got a lovely pair of eyes,' says Dai.

When it comes to teachers, Peri's something else. Her real name's Miss Rhiannon Jenkins and she lives a mile down the road, on a sheep farm. She always wears trousers and boots, because she only works part-time and she's always dashing back home to her farm. She's a dab hand at the shearing; maybe that's why we've never seen her in a skirt. One day, she wore a pair of grey jeans to school and Mr Beynon stopped her in the corridor.

'Miss Jenkins,' he boomed at her, 'I do not actually forbid trousers to female members of staff, but I do frown on them.'

That didn't rattle Peri's maracas any. 'I'm not a member of your staff,' she said. 'I'm peripatetic, part-time.' She gives him a big smile and walks away. That's what Merco told us, anyway.

'There's no such word,' said Emma, 'she must of said pathetic.'

'No,' said Merco. 'She said peripatetic. I heard it clearly.'

'Maybe that's her nickname' said Emma.

'Peripatetic isn't a nickname,' says Andrea. 'They're short, nicknames.'

So we call her Peri, for short.

When we get to music, Peri's got a visitor: Mr Dylan James from Metalwork. He keeps sheep too.

'You're early,' Peri tells us. 'Sit over there and talk quietly. We won't be long.' And she goes back to her conversation. They're discussing the current price of sheep-dip and a forthcoming sheep-dog trial. Mr James wants to know if Peri's going to Lampeter next weekend.

'We'll see,' says Peri. 'It's only Monday yet. Lot of water to go under the fridge before the weekend. I'll be in again on Friday. Sound me out then, Dylan.' She gives him a big smile and he turns to us.

'Make sure you behave for Miss Jenkins,' he says. 'She may only be peripatetic, but she's an asset to this school. An asset.'

'Silly old fool,' says Peri, after Mr James goes out.

'We thought you fancied him, Miss,' says Andrea.

'Then just you think again,' says Peri. 'Right, everyone. Pull your chairs up. I want to do some rhythm work with you.'

'Aren't we going to play the clarinet?' wails Emma.

'You tell me,' says Peri. 'Can you get a note out yet?'

'No,' says Emma.

'Well, keep practising at home,' says Peri. 'Meantime, we'll learn to read notes in anticipation of the day you're able to play them.' She draws a treble clef on the board. 'Four beats to the bar,' she says. 'Crochet for Dai and two quavers for Emma, because she talks twice as fast as he does.'

'You talking Russian?' asks Andrea

'Try it,' says Peri, chanting, 'Dai, Dai, Emma, Emma,' and clapping the rhythm. Then she writes it on the board.

We soon get the hang of it, marching round the room chanting and clapping 'Dai Dai Emma Dai' and 'Emma Emma Dai Dai', and Peri beating time on a tambourine.

We're still chanting when Merco Rigger comes to the door with an envelope for Miss Peri. He takes one look at us, grins, and joins in the marching.

'It's good here,' says Emma. 'Want to join us, and learn the clarinet?'

'No thanks,' says Merco. 'No time.'

'Make time,' says Peri. 'I'm always on the look-out for new pupils. Wouldn't you like to learn an instrument?'

'I can nearly play a note now,' says Emma. '*And* you misses Geography.'

'I do that already,' says Merco. 'And I can play the clarinet, too.'

'Oh,' says Peri, looking at him sideways and smiling, 'you can, can you?'

'Yes,' says Merc, 'I can.'

'Play us a tune then, Merc,' she says, handing him a clarinet.

Merco looks at the group. 'I don't want to put them off, Miss,' he says. 'When they hears how good I am, they'll all give up.'

We're all laughing now.

'I think we'll cope,' says Peri. 'Go on, Merco, boy. Put your mouth where your money is.'

He picks up the clarinet, fixes his lips and starts to play. He doesn't puff out his cheeks and you can't hear him taking a breath. You can't hear us taking a breath either. The hinges have fallen off our jaws and we're staring at Merco like we've never seen him before. Whatever he's playing, it's smooth as honey and light as a dandelion seed. It makes me want to cry.

When he puts down the clarinet, Peri's voice comes out slow motion. 'Where did you learn to play like that, boy?'

'Oh, I just picked it up,' said Merc, putting the clarinet down on the table and hurrying off to catch up on his messages.

Dai's Gran Comes to Parents' Evening

We've been getting ready for Parents' Evening all week. We've been putting charts on the walls, covering exercise books with wallpaper and tidying the classroom. Pietro's making labels for posters on WAR - WHO NEEDS IT? and SYMMETRY IN NATURE, and Ceri and Rhodri are fixing them to the wall. Even Dai Rix is busy, doing his homework corrections at last.

'More sticky tape,' says Ceri. Byron Huw Tapper hands him a new roll.

'All this fuss for one day,' sighs Rhodri.

The girls are practising for the SHORT CONCERT TO ROUND OFF THE EVENING. We're singing Songs From the Shows. There's one called 'I feel pretty' and the boys are all singing a rather rude word instead of 'pretty'.

'Your Mam coming tonight?' asks Andrea, as we tidy books in the library.

'Yes,' I say. 'She's leaving work early. Your Mam coming?'

'She's taking it in turns with my Nan to look after the baby. Mam's coming for the plastic tea and Nan's coming for the singing.'

'Your Mam dressing up?'

'They're all dressing up,' sighs Andrea.

I watch Dai altering all the marks in his Maths book. He changes a three to an eight and a one to a seven.

'I can change the numbers,' he says, 'but not the writing? Look what Mrs Flynn's written. *Dai, this is NOT the right way to do fractions. See me.*'

'You could change *not* to *now*,' I say, 'then it'll say *this is NOW the right way to do fractions.*'

'Ace,' says Dai. 'Thanks, Nia.'

'What will Mrs Flynn say when she sees what you've done?'

'Nothing to what my Nan will say if she sees low marks,' says Dai. 'She thinks I'm top of the class.'

'You, top of class? Why does she think that?'

'Because I told her I was,' says Dai.

Dai lives with his Nan, Mrs Ethel Rix, in a stone house surrounded by rose bushes. She makes Dai wash the dishes and weed the garden and help with the shopping. I often see Dai with his Nan in the supermarket. She makes him push the trolley round and reach for topshelf goods. If it wasn't for her fussing, he'd sit watching television all day and all night.

At four o'clock, Emma Leyshon and I have to go down to the Head's room to help Miss Mair Owen serve teas to the Governors and Councillors. The room looks different from normal, with lace-covered tables and china tea-sets. There are sandwiches without crusts and cream cakes on silver stands.

'Ready for the VIP's, girls?' says Miss Mair Owen. 'Make sure you fix smiles before they come in, won't you?'

Mr Beynon arrives, alone, to check there's no dust on the carpet. He looks at his watch. 'Shall I bring them in now, Miss Mair Owen?' he asks.

'Anchors away, Headmaster,' she says.

He turns to Emma, 'Ready to dispense cream cakes?' he asks. She nods.

'Sandwiches separated for ease of selection?' he asks me. I nod, too.

'I shall bring the Councillors in now,' he announces, 'followed by the School Governors. Please ensure that you give the Councillors their tea first.'

As soon as he closes the door, Miss Mair Owen has a fit of giggles. You'd think she'd be used to the way he talks, being his secretary. But she repeats. 'Sandwiches separated for ease of selection' several times before she stops laughing.

'They call it Parents' Day,' she says, when she calms down, 'but they're not the important ones, are they? Just look at this spread. Your parents just get weak tea in plastic beakers and one free ginger biscuit.'

The door opens and Mr Beynon ushers in a load of pressed suits and tailored costumes. Miss Mair Owen pours tea into china cups and we help her hand them to the Councillors and Governors. Then Emma and I take plates of sandwiches round the tables, making sure everyone's got enough to eat.

When I get to the table nearest the door, I'm surprised to see Dai Rix's Grandma sitting there. She's wearing a large green hat with cherries on it.

'Hello, Mrs Rix,' I say. 'I like your hat.'

'Nia, isn't it? Yes, done me proud, this hat has. Bought it in 1985, for the funeral. Worn it everywhere since. Senior Citizens Outings, School Fetes. What's in the sandwiches, Nia love?'

'White sandwiches, ham with pickle, cheese with chives, cucumber with prawn; brown ones, egg mayonnaise with watercress and salmon with tomato.'

She takes one of each and places them carefully on her plate.

'I didn't know you were a councillor,' I say.

'I'm not,' she says, taking a bite out of an egg mayonnaise sandwich.

'A governor? Dai never said,' I say.

'I'm not that, neither,' she grins at me. 'I just followed this lot in. Can't stand tea in plastic cups. No-one's said a thing. The Governors think I'm a Councillor, the Councillors think I'm a Governor and that Headmaster is too busy feeding the Chairman's face to notice me. Get us another cup of tea will you, love?'

Later, all the suits and costumes go off to the SHORT CONCERT.

'Come on, Nia,' says Emma, 'we got to sing.'

'You go,' I say, 'I'll be there in a minute.'

Miss Mair Owen makes strong cups of tea for herself and Mrs Rix and a weak tea for me. We help ourselves to sandwiches.

'You're missing the concert,' I tell them.

'That's good,' says Miss Mair Owen. 'I've heard them rehearsing all week.'

'Don't you want to go to the concert?' I ask Dai's Gran.

'No, thank you, love,' she says. 'I'll stay here

with you, if that's alright. I'm having such a lovely time.'

'But you won't see Dai's books,' I say.

Mrs Rix bites into a cucumber sandwich and smiles. 'I know,' she says. 'This is a lot more fun.'

Growing up

The doorbell rings.

'It's Andrea for you,' says my Mum. 'She wants you to go for a walk. She's got the baby with her. Don't be long now: there's a pile of ironing waiting.'

Andrea's got Leah in the buggy. She smiles at me, Leah, and then says 'Neenee'.

'She knows you,' says Andrea, surprised.

'Well, of course she knows me. I'm always round your house.'

'No, I mean she knows your name. She said Neenee.'

'My name's Nia,' I say, 'not neenee. And anyway, she can't talk.'

'Yes she can,' says Andrea. She smiles at Leah. 'Say Dada,' she says.

'Dada, Baba, Indi, Neenee.'

'See,' says Andrea.

'She can talk,' I say, surprised. 'When did that happen?'

'Yesterday,' said Andrea. 'When I came home from school, she smiled at me and said Indi. That's what she calls me, Indi. Funny, isn't it?

One day she can't talk, the next she can. She'll be ringing her boyfriend on the telephone tomorrow.'

I laugh. 'We don't even do that,' I say.

It's getting dark when we round the corner of the street and look up at Glantwrch sprouting like a black mushroom at the top of the hill. Andrea puts the brake on the buggy and we sit on a low wall watching Leah sleeping in the shadows from Middle School.

'I remember when she slept all day and couldn't even focus,' I say.

'Can't hold back progress,' says Andrea, Beynon-style. 'One day, we'll be sitting here with our own babies.'

I look at Andrea and laugh. 'Can you imagine it,' I say, 'holding hands with some boy? Going sloppy? Who do you fancy, Andrea? Dai?'

But Andrea doesn't laugh back. She sits there, staring at her feet. Then she turns round, and blurts out, 'I gotta boyfriend.'

'You have? You? Who?' I sound like an owl.

'I wanted to tell you for weeks.'

'For weeks? Who?'

'We've been to the pictures twice now. It's Pietro.'

I breathe a sigh of relief. It's only Pietro.

'We've been kissing.'

'You have? You? Kissing?'

I look up to the school to see if it's still there. Then I say again 'Kissing?' I don't sound so shocked this time. I can get used to this.

'We're going to be an item, me and Pietro. That's what I wanted to tell you. Holding hands in school. And things.'

'You? But . . .' There's no words for this situation. 'Why?'

Andrea looks at Leah. 'She'll be walking soon,' she says. 'It just happens. Things happen to you and you can't do anything about it. One day, I was saying *Boys, who needs them*, and the next day I just wanted to kiss Pietro back. It happens.'

'What about us?' I ask. 'Are we still going to be friends?'

'Of course we are,' said Andrea. 'When you gets a boyfriend, we'll all go out together. It's just . . . well, Pietro will be picking me up for school in the mornings. Things like that.'

I sit on my own a while, when Andrea's gone, looking up at the school.

'Hi, Nia.' It's Merc. 'What are you doing?'

I look at Merc and try to imagine kissing. It's just not possible.

'Gotta go,' I say. 'There's a pile of ironing waiting in the kitchen.'